Pinocchio

Twin Books

LONGMEADOW
PRESS

Once upon a time, in a sleepy little village in Italy, there lived a small fellow named Jiminy Cricket. Now, Jiminy loved to travel from hearth to hearth, singing as he went. And one night, when the wishing star hung bright in the velvet sky, Jiminy visited the home of the woodcarver, Geppetto.

Geppetto's workshop was a magical place. There were cuckoo clocks and music boxes that tinkled merrily. There were ducks and geese and puppets all made of wood. And there were endless shelves of toys.

The kindly woodcarver loved to make children smile, and so each toy was made with special care. But there was one toy more colorfully painted than the rest – a boy puppet made of wood. It sat on the workshop table, still needing a few finishing touches.

Geppetto stood before the puppet and carefully painted on eyebrows and a mouth. His cat, Figaro, and his goldfish, Cleo, looked on.

"Now," said Geppetto, "I have just the name for you – Pinocchio! Do you like it, Figaro?"

Figaro shook his furry head.

"No? Well, you will grow to like it," said Geppetto. "'Pinocchio' it is."

Later that evening,
Geppetto put Pinocchio
away for the night and
climbed into bed. Before he
fell asleep, Geppetto looked
out his window at the
brightly lit sky.

"Oh, Figaro – look!" he
exclaimed. "The Wishing
Star!"

Geppetto made a wish. It was one dear to his heart. "Star light, star bright. First star I see tonight. I wish I may, I wish I might have the wish I wish tonight!

"Figaro, do you know what I wished? I wished that my little Pinocchio might be a real boy," said Geppetto. Then he settled into bed.

While the village slept, a brilliant light of palest blue filled Geppetto's workshop. The beautiful light sparkled and transformed itself into the Blue Fairy.

"Good Geppetto," said the fairy to the sleeping man, "you have given so much happiness to others. You deserve to have your wish come true!"

The Blue Fairy glided across the room to Pinocchio. She lifted her golden wand and waved it through the air. "Little puppet made of pine, wake! The gift of life is thine!" she proclaimed.

As Jiminy Cricket
watched, Pinocchio opened
his eyes. He moved first one
arm, then the other. Then he
opened his mouth. "I can
move!" said Pinocchio,
excited. "I can talk!"

"Yes, Pinocchio," said the
Blue Fairy, "I have given
you life because tonight
Geppetto wished for a real
boy."

"Am I a real boy?" asked
Pinocchio.

"No, Pinocchio," said the
fairy. "You may be a real
boy someday. But first, you
must prove yourself brave,
truthful and unselfish. You
must learn to choose
between right and wrong."

"But how will I know?"
asked Pinocchio.

"Let your conscience be your guide," said the fairy.

"What is a conscience?" asked Pinocchio.

"What is a conscience?" repeated Jiminy Cricket. "I'll tell you! A conscience is that still, small voice that people won't listen to. That's just the trouble with the world today," said Jiminy, jabbing his umbrella in the air.

"Mr. Cricket," said the fairy, "would you like to be Pinocchio's conscience?"

"Well – uh, well I, uh-huh – sure!"

So the fairy named him Sir Jiminy cricket, lord of the knowledge of right and wrong. Then she was gone.

Geppetto heard voices and got out of bed. As he came into his workshop, he could hardly believe his eyes. Right before him was his puppet, dancing about and singing.

"Can I be dreaming? My little Pinocchio is a real boy!" Geppetto cried. The gentle woodcarver lifted Pinocchio into the air and hugged the wooden boy close to him. "Oh, thank you, Wishing Star, for making my wish come true!"

20

"Figaro, look! He's alive!" said Geppetto. "But how?"

Pinocchio happily explained all about the visit of the Blue Fairy.

"A real boy!" whispered Geppetto. "It's my wish come true! Cleo, isn't that wonderful?" Cleo leaped out of her bowl excitedly and Figaro joined in the celebration. Then, after a while, they all went back to bed.

The next morning after breakfast, Geppetto walked outside with Pinocchio and handed him some books.

"What are these for, Father?" asked Pinocchio.

Geppetto pointed to the children passing by. "Do you see those children? They are going to school. Now that you are a little boy and not a puppet, you must also go to school," Geppetto explained.

With an apple in one hand and his schoolbooks in the other, Pinocchio hurried off in search of the school. He wanted to be like all the other boys and girls.

"I'll make Father proud," he said, gaily swinging his books and whistling.

Pinocchio walked through the village, quite unaware that he was being watched by two very suspicious-looking characters.

"Look at that!" the fox exclaimed. "A live puppet without strings! We can make a fortune if we sell him to Stromboli for the puppet show." The fox rubbed his paws together greedily.

As Pinocchio walked by, the fox tripped him with his cane.

"Oh, I'm terribly sorry!" apologized the fox. "Allow me to introduce myself. I am J. Worthington Foulfellow, but my friends call me Honest John," he said with a bow.

"And this is my friend Gideon," he added, pointing to the cat standing beside him.

"How do you do?" replied Pinocchio politely. "I must go. I'm in a terrible hurry."

"And where are you going?" asked Honest John.

"Why, to school, of course," answered Pinocchio.

"School!" sneered the fox. "Why waste your time going to school? A talented boy like you should be on the stage."

"Do you mean, be an actor?" asked Pinocchio with wonder.

"Yes, just think of it – bright lights, music, the roar of applause – and fame!" Gideon nodded his head in agreement. "Come with us," said the fox slyly. "We'll make you a star."

Meanwhile, back at Geppetto's workshop, Jiminy Cricket was just waking up. "Whooo," said Jiminy, hurrying into his hat and coat, "fine conscience I turned out to be – late the first day!" He fixed his tie, buttoned his vest, and ran out the door.

"Oh well," said Jiminy, racing after Pinocchio, "he can't get into much trouble between here and school."

But just then, Jiminy saw Honest John and Gideon leading Pinocchio down the street – in the wrong direction.

33

"Hey!" called Jiminy. "Hold on there!" But Pinocchio didn't hear him.

Jiminy yelled a little louder. "Hey! Pinoke! Where you goin'?"

"Oh, hello, Jiminy," said Pinocchio. "I'm going to be an actor."

"What?" asked Jiminy. "Now wait a minute, son. You can't go to the theater. Here's what you do," explained Jiminy. "You say thank you just the same, you're sorry, but you've got to go to school."

"Right" said Pinocchio.

"Pinocchio! Oh, Pinocchiooo!" called Honest John. "Yoo-hoo!"

Pinocchio heard his name, forgot all about Jiminy Cricket and walked right into Stromboli's wagon.

When Stromboli saw Pinocchio, he rubbed his hands together with glee. *A puppet with no strings!* thought Stromboli. *He will make me lots of money!*

That evening, Pinocchio made his stage debut. Jiminy Cricket had followed Pinocchio, and now he sat in the theater watching. Everyone seemed amazed to see a puppet without strings.

When the show was over, the crowd applauded and threw gold coins at Pinocchio's feet.

"Huh!" said Jiminy, impressed. "They like him!" The applause continued as Stromboli joined Pinocchio on stage. Pinocchio loved all the attention. He was stage-struck!

Meanwhile, Geppetto was very worried. When nightfall came, he and Figaro went out to search for the missing Pinocchio.

"What could have happened to him?" asked Geppetto, swinging his lantern. "Where could he be at this hour? Pinocchio!" Geppetto called out until his throat was sore. "PINOCCHIO!"

But by sunrise, Geppetto still had not found him.

41

Back at Stromboli's, Pinocchio was in trouble. Stromboli threatened to use him as firewood if he didn't behave, then locked Pinocchio in a cage.

That night, Jiminy Cricket sneaked into the room. "Pinocchio!" said Jiminy, surprised to find his friend locked up. "What's happened?"

Pinocchio explained, sobbing.

"Don't worry, son" said Jiminy, hopping up to the cage. "Why, I'll have you out in no time."

Jiminy tried and tried, but he just could not get that lock to open. He had finally given up when a dazzling blue light filled the room.

"The Blue Fairy!" whispered Jiminy.

"Pinocchio, why didn't you go to school?" asked the fairy.

"School? Well, I – uh," Pinocchio thought quickly. "I was going to school till I met somebody."

"Met somebody?" asked the fairy.

"Yeah! Uh – two big monsters. And – and they tied me in a big sack!"

Pinocchio was lying, of course, and with each lie, his nose grew and grew, until it stretched through the bars of the cage.

"You see, Pinocchio, a lie keeps growing and growing until it's as plain as the nose on your face," explained the Blue Fairy.

"I'll never lie again. Honest, I won't," promised Pinocchio, trembling with fear.

Jiminy Cricket cleared his throat. "Please, your honor – uh-uh, I mean, Miss Fairy. Give him another chance," he pleaded.

Since Pinocchio was genuinely sorry, the Blue Fairy waved her magic wand and unlocked the cage.

"I'll forgive you this once, but remember: a boy who won't be good might just as well be made of wood."

"Oh, I'll be good!" insisted Pinocchio.

"Very well," said the fairy. Then she disappeared. Jiminy and Pinocchio jumped down from the cage.

"Come on, my boy," said Jiminy Cricket. "Let's go!"

In a nearby tavern, Honest John and Gideon sat with the Coachman. These three scoundrels were finishing up the details of a deal.

Now the Coachman was an evil man who lured naughty boys to Pleasure Island to make silly donkeys of themselves. Once there, the boys never returned home. Honest John and Gideon agreed to help the Coachman find some more boys.

Filling their pockets with gold coins, Honest John and Gideon went searching for bad little boys. They had barely stepped outside when they spotted Pinocchio.

Honest John stuck out his cane and pulled Pinocchio aside. "Hello, young man," said Honest John, tipping his hat." And where are you off to now?"

"I'm going home to Father," stammered the startled puppet.

"You look a bit pale. Let me check your pulse," said the fox, holding Pinocchio's wrist.

"Ah! Just as I thought. You can't possibly go home in this condition. What you need is rest and relaxation. I know just the spot," he chuckled. "Pleasure Island."

"Pleasure Island?" asked Pinocchio.

"Trust me," said Honest John slyly. "It's a wonderful place."

Once again the two rascals
led Pinocchio down the
street. They filled his head
with promises of games and
toys, and all the candy he
could eat.

Jiminy Cricket followed at
a distance. "This doesn't
look too good to me," he
groaned. "I don't know how
he's ever going to get to be a
real boy following those two
around."

"Where are they taking him now?" wondered Jiminy.

Outside the village, Foulfellow handed Pinocchio over to the Coachman. The excited puppet climbed on to the stagecoach, which was already filled with laughing, chattering boys.

The Coachman cracked his whip and the stagecoach began its journey to Pleasure Island.

By nightfall, they were on the ferry that would take them to Pleasure Island. During the crossing, Pinocchio met a boy named Lampwick.

"Ever been to Pleasure Island?" asked Lampwick.

"Uh-uh," answered Pinocchio.

"Me neither," said Lampwick, "but they say it's a swell joint. No school, you loaf around, plenty to eat, plenty to drink - and it's free!"

"Look at all those cigars!" cried Pinocchio as the ferry came to a stop.

"This is it!" yelled Lampwick. The boys ran down the gangplank on to the mysterious island.

"If my mother could see me now, she'd have a fit," laughed Lampwick, getting ready to bite into a gigantic sandwich. "On Pleasure Island I can eat whatever I want. Do you want a bite?" he asked.

Pinocchio shook his head. He was busy enough trying to eat a lollipop and a candy cane at the same time.

While Pinocchio stuffed himself with sweets, Jiminy Cricket explored the island. He crept up behind the Coachman, who was giving orders to his men.

"As soon as those brats turn into donkeys, I want you to round them up. They should be down in the salt mines by daybreak!" yelled the Coachman, cracking his whip.

"So that's it," said Jiminy, frightened. "I'd better find Pinocchio!" Jiminy held on to his hat and raced off to warn his friend.

Jiminy found Pinocchio in the pool hall with Lampwick. He told Pinocchio what he had just heard. The two boys began to laugh.

"You take orders from a grasshopper?" Lampwick snickered.

"All right!" said the
indignant Jiminy. "Go on –
laugh – make donkeys out of
yourselves! See if I care," he
added, stomping off.

The two boys continued to giggle as Lampwick made fun of Jiminy. "You'd think something terrible was going to happen," laughed Lampwick.

No sooner had he said this than he sprouted donkey's ears. Pinocchio stared in horror as Lampwick also grew a tail, and his feet turned into hooves.

Lampwick went on laughing, not noticing what was happening.

Suddenly, Lampwick's laugh turned into a hee-haw.
"Did that come out of me?" he brayed.

Pinocchio nodded.

Then Lampwick felt his face and chin, and his long,
furry ears. "Oooh!" Lampwick cried, for he had indeed
become a donkey. He galloped around the pool room in
a panic.

Suddenly Pinocchio saw that he, too, had sprouted
donkey's ears and a tail. "Jiminy! Jiminy – help!"
screamed Pinocchio.

Jiminy Cricket rushed into the room, shocked at what
he found.

"Quick! We've got to get out of here!" yelled Jiminy.

Pinocchio and Jiminy Cricket raced across the now-deserted island, leaping over mounds of discarded candy and toys. They ran as fast as they possible could.

"Faster, Pinocchio! We must get off this island before daybreak," urged Jiminy.

When they reached the edge of the island, they found themselves at a cliff overlooking the sea.

"You've got to jump!" yelled Jiminy. So Pinocchio dove in and Jiminy followed, using his umbrella as a parachute.

Because Pinocchio was made of wood, he immediately floated to the surface and stayed there. The cricket jumped on his back and the current carried them toward the mainland.

The bedraggled pair reached the shore at sunrise. "I sure made a mess of things," moaned Pinocchio. "Now I'll never become a real boy."

Nearby, Jiminy noticed a floating bottle. "Pinocchio!" called the cricket. "Grab that bottle. There's a message in it."

Pinocchio reached for the bottle and gave it to Jiminy, who read the message. "It says Geppetto was headed for Pleasure Island when Monstro the Whale swallowed his boat. But Geppetto is still alive in his belly."

"I must save Father from that nasty whale," said Pinocchio, running toward the water.

"Wait!" yelled Jiminy. "You can't go underwater. You're made of wood and you'll float."

"Not if I use this to weigh me down," replied Pinocchio, tying a rock to his tail and jumping into the water.

At the bottom of the ocean, Jiminy and Pinocchio began their search for Monstro and Geppetto.

Suddenly they swam into an enormous shadow that covered the ocean floor. Pinocchio and Jiminy looked up, terrified to see Monstro looming above them.

Pinocchio untied the stone and floated up toward the whale. At that moment, Monstro opened his gigantic jaws, ready to eat lunch. He sucked in a whole school of fish, as well as the struggling Pinocchio.

Jiminy banged on the wale's closed teeth, yelling, "Open up, Blubbermouth! I've got to get in there!"

Pinocchio swam with the fish down the whale's throat to its cavern-like belly. When he got there, he saw Geppetto and Figaro fishing from the side of their boat.

When Geppetto pulled in his net, he had quite a surprise. "Pinocchio!" cried the woodcarver. "My son!" Gepetto hugged Pinocchio to his chest.

"Father," declared Pinocchio, "I have come to save you!"

"Oh, no, son! No. It's quite hopeless, I'm afraid."

"We must get out of here," insisted Pinocchio, "but how?"

"Pinocchio?" Geppetto asked suddenly. "What has happened to your ears?"

"I'll explain later," said Pinocchio. "There's no time now." Pinocchio began breaking up furniture. He had an idea.

"We'll start a fire and make lots of smoke. Then Monstro will wake up and sneeze us out."

Monstro soon began to feel the fire in his belly. He tossed and turned frantically, hurling his gigantic body through the waves. Inside, the captives quickly jumped on to a raft and paddled toward the whale's throat.

"Hurry, Father!" yelled Pinocchio.

"We'll never get by those teeth," murmured Gepetto.

"Yes we will!" Pinocchio assured him.

When they reached the whale's mouth, his gigantic teeth barred their way. But then Monstro let out an enormous sneeze, blowing the raft out to sea.

When Jiminy Cricket saw the raft coming, he hopped on.

"Hang on!" shouted Pinocchio. "Here we go!"

Even though they were free, they were not yet out of danger. Monstro was furious. Seeing the raft bobbing up ahead, he nose-dived under the water.

For an instant it seemed he had disappeared, but then his giant tail flipped up under the raft and tossed it into the air, smashing it to pieces.

As Geppetto began to sink, Pinocchio grabbed him and carried him on his back.

"Swim for shore! Save yourself," the old man moaned, gasping for air.

Eventually they were washed up on shore. Geppetto looked around to see if everyone was there. To his dismay, he saw Pinocchio lying face-down in the water.

"My brave little boy," Geppetto cried, lifting the still body into his arms. The sad group stumbled back to the village.

Geppetto laid Pinocchio on his bed and knelt by his side. "Little Pinocchio, you risked your life to save me," sobbed the old man, lowering his head in sorrow.

All of a sudden, the room was lit up by a brilliant blue light. The Blue Fairy appeared. Waving her magic wand over Pinocchio, she said, "Now you have proven yourself brave, truthful and unselfish. Today you will become a real boy. Awake, Pinocchio, awake!"

The lifeless wooden boy was suddenly transformed into a real live little boy.

Sitting up, Pinocchio blinked his eyes. "Why are you crying, Papa?" he asked.

"Pinocchio! You're alive," gasped Geppetto with joy. "And you're a real, live boy."

Cleo jumped with joy and Figaro danced a jig. At last the gentle woodcarver's wish had come true.

Jiminy Cricket watched the joyous scene. "Now I know that wishes *do* sometimes come true," he said with tears in his eyes.

This edition produced for
Longmeadow Press
by Twin Books Corp

Copyright © 1986, 1991 The Walt Disney Company

ISBN 0-681-41427-8

Printed in Hong Kong